To Joyce
I Am
Time was
was at t.

MW01532663

Butch

Short Tales

Other titles by this author

Deutschtown's Pigeon Hill

Smelling Lilac

Missing Doris

Short Tales

Ambrose E. Korn Jr.

ISBN: 978-1-257-63269-5

PublishNation LLC
www.publishnation.net

Acknowledgements

Riley Wilbert for Computer Assistance

Short Stories

Tet

**Gunnery Sergeant John (Red Dog) Paul
"Miss You Buddy"**

***Tet, the Vietnamese lunar new year holiday,
fell on the last day of January, 1968.***

*The Viet Cong had announced a countrywide Tet truce for January
27-February 3. In return South Vietnamese also agreed to a cease
fire. On January 29 the truce was violated. Da Nang was attacked.
Hue was attacked. By January 31 most major cities, military bases
in South Vietnam were being attacked by North Vietnam regular
soldiers and the Viet Cong guerillas.*

1

Preface to Tet

With as few words as possible I wanted to highlight three observations about the Vietnam war. First, the war was fought mostly by young men from working class families, slum area youth, and the heroic do or die educated fighter pilots from all branches of the military.

Second, all of the airmen prisoners of war held at the Hanoi Hilton and shot down over North Vietnam were ordered on missions selected by President Johnson and his administration. Most tactically useless missions flown by brave A4 Navy/Marine Corps Pilots off of carriers or Air Force Thud Pilots flying out of Thailand. Those that are interested can find many recordings of documentation on U-tube about many of their senseless missions and told by the pilots themselves. Google the return of the American prisoners of war and you will see that all of the released prisoners of war were airmen.

And third, there is a reason for that; The fighting in South Vietnam with the exception of a few battles as the tet offensive was guerilla warfare. Ambushes fought in the jungle by rice farmers and part-time Viet Cong fighters. Fighters continuously supplied by communist North Vietnam who in turn were being supplied by Russian ships in harbors American Pilots were ordered not to bomb by Johnson. The enemy jungle fighters in South Vietnam took no prisoners. They couldn't. What could they do with them? Take them home for dinner! Viet Cong survivors from a firefight returning to their village hid their weapon and picked up a hoe.

Lessons learned: For a guerrilla, or irregular force to be successful it needs three components. It needs men willing to fight and die; It needs supporters to continuously supply them with arms and munitions, and it needs safe places to take sanctuary. Take one component away and they lose. The Viet Cong had all three necessities.

They had men willing to die. They had continuous safe supply lines from Russia and China. They had sanctuary when necessary in neighboring nations such as Laos, and the demilitarized zone was regularly violated by the communists. And our own president imposed bombing restrictions on our airmen.

When President Nixon got elected he ordered the bombing of the Ho Chi Minh trail in the country of Laos and the main support line supplying the Viet Cong Guerillas. He authorized some bombing of enemy harbors. He ordered the main harbor Haiphong mined and a Naval blockade. After those actions the Communist North Vietnamese agreed to the Paris Peace Accords.

Unfortunately after a time, and with most American forces withdrawn, the Regular North Vietnamees Army attacked the south in mass and was victorious.

Tet

Tet Attack at Cam Lo

It was daybreak when the CH46 made a rapid circling descent, straightened out and came to a hover over the Landing Zone. Captain Benzer could see a Corpsman on the ground struggling to place a dead Marine into a body bag. As the helicopter touched down the dusty air kicked up by the spinning rotor blades blew a poncho covering off of a dead Marine. The young face with eyes closed looked asleep.The Captain kept looking through the dust swirling air at the still face and thought of the Marine's family. They would be going about their routine lives and not yet knowing he is dead. It always grieved him when thinking of the fallen men and their families. A lifetime of grief awaited that Marine's family, and somewhere a Marine Officer would have to make notification to the next-of-kin of that young face in his sight. He thought he'd rather be where he was than to be that officer knocking on the dead Marine's hometown door like the Grim Reaper himself.

Close to the Landing Zone and standing by more poncho-covered bodies he spotted Sergeant Major Smoky waiting to greet and brief him on the overnight battle. He already knew that one of the covered bodies was the Compound Commander who was killed soon after the battle began. Only one other junior officer was posted at the compound and that young lieutenant leaned mightily on Smoky to get through the nighttime attack until he too was wounded and Smoky took command. The Captain jumped from the chopper and rushed to the saluting sergeant. He returned his salute. The smell of the night battle was still in the morning air.

They walked away from the noisy helicopter toward the northwest corner of the compound. Before they got there another CH46 was lifting off with WIA and KIA for Da Nang. Reaching the northwest corner the two Marines watched as enlisted men pulled and tugged and yanked dead NVA and VC bodies off of the wires. Smoky spoke first.

"There Are three rows of wire around the compound and in some places they penetrated into the third row. Determined little bastards."

"Body count yet?"

"Marines, KIA 10, WIA 17."

They both lit a cigarette while watching the grunts gathering the bodies off of the wire.

"NVA?"

Smoky shook his helmeted head. Counting these over 100. You know how they are; digging graves before night attacks so they can quickly bury their dead. After a while I'll send a patrol out to look for body dragging trails. I expect more to be dragged to their graves on the other side of our wires."

The longtime friends puffed away watching the grunts lay the enemy dead in a row not far from where they smoked. Both were dressed in the same battle gear as the men under their command. One NVA body bent over the wire was facing away from the compound as if trying to retreat and the Marines were cursing as they struggled to yank him loose from the wire. After a strong tug on the North Vietnamese soldier's legs his pants slid off revealing human waste. The two Marines jumped backwards with one calling out to the others. "This one shit himself."

Smoky instructed. "They're scared shitless just like everyone else in battle and it's nothing to be moping over if you shit your own pants last night." The Sergeant Major dropped his cigarette butt and stomped on it with his heavy boot. "Now get that stinking communist hero off of our wire."

The Captain flicked his smoking butt away and stared at it arcing through the air and turned to Smoky. How the hell did we get here?"

The Sergeant Major grinned. "I reckon it was that train we boarded out of Pittsburgh in 55" He continued answering. "Running from our teenage distress?"

Captain Bat didn't answer. It was more than 2 years since he was commissioned into the officer corps and Smoky had advanced to the top of the enlisted ranks. Both knew that the Vietnam war had as much to do with their advancement in the Marines as their excellent hard earned record as Marines. The war caused Congress to expand the size of the Corps and with that expansion experienced Marines were promoted to fill the leadership positions that came with the mushrooming build up of the ranks. They left the body count and walked toward the command post talking and thinking on their first encounter as teenagers.

* * * * *

The impressively lit street entry rotunda of the Pennsylvania Train Station was glistening in the drizzling rain shower. Beams of light from the circling automobiles dropping off or picking up passengers reflected across the wet brown brick turnaround and corner tower pavilions. Above the early twentieth century structure a large center skylight circled with clear glass electric bulbs illuminated the atrium below.

Bat Benzer's buddy from his corner drugstore gang dropped him off under the rotunda. He watched his friend drive away into Pittsburgh's city lights before turning away and entering the station's grand concourse. Only seventeen years old he didn't wander far away from the station entrance to await the Marine Corps recruiting sergeant. He was early. It was ten o'clock and the train he would board to begin his journey to Parris Island wasn't scheduled to depart until near to midnight.

A teenager sitting on a wooden bench next to a row of telephone booths beckoned for Bat to join him on the bench. On the floor under the bench was a small canvas handbag similar in size to the bag Bat carried. He approached the smiling lad.

"Took a guess and waved reckoning y'all waiting for the Marine recruiter too?"

"You're right."

"Sit a spell. Folks call me Smoky."

Bat sat next to the teen. "Bat."

"Where?" Smoky asked, looking about the concourse.

"That's my name. Short for Bartholomew."

"Seems they'd be calling you Bart?"

"I was told when my German grandpa said Bart it sounded like Bat and it stuck. I don't remember being called anything else."

Smoky smiled and extended his hand. "Never took the hand of a bat before."

They shook hands.

"Your clothes are wet." Bat said. "Get caught in the rain shower?"

"Yep I did. Walking from the Greyhound Bus Station. I got a dry shirt in my tote bag but figured I'll keep it till further along on the trip.

"I thought you might be from out of town. You talk differently."

8

"I enlisted in Weirton, about forty miles as the crow flies. Recruiters around the West Virginia Panhandle bus recruits to Pittsburgh to catch the train. What about you?

"I live here in Pittsburgh." Bat answered with a question of his own. "You live in Weirton?"

"I was raised in the Smoky Mountains. Most of my kin still live between Gatlinburg Tennessee and Bluefield West Virginia. A few years back my folks came north cuz my Pa got a job with Weirton Steel. He was getting breathing problems and didn't want to coal mine any more. But I still go back to the Smoky's visiting kin."

"Is that how you got your name?"

"Yep. And that's my Christian name. My Pa gave it to me so I'd never forget where I come from."

They sat quietly looking around the concourse and thinking about some topic to keep the conversation going between them. Smoky spoke his thoughts.

"Folks in Weirton talk like folks around here in Pittsburgh. I went to two years of high school in Weirton and was told I talk like a hillbilly. Cause I grew up hearing Smoky mountain slang. Then I go back to the Smoky Mountains." He paused. "They say I talk like a Yankee. I'm odd. I recollect as odd as a blue eyed bat"

"Then I'm odd too." Bat chuckled. "Or haven't you noticed I have blue eyes."

Smoky slapped his knee. "My first time visiting home, I swear, I'm telling my folks I finally saw a blue eyed bat and slap my hand on the family Bible if need be."

Bat laughed with Smoky. He was glad they connected and would journey together. "You feel nervous about going to Parris Island? I heard it's tough. I hope I get through the training okay."

"My Pa and my uncle told me what's gonna happen. We'll be in a peck of trouble for a time, running about like chickens with heads cut off. Your bushy hairy noggin Bat will be made bald. That's why I got my hair snipped down to my dome. And don't take much stuff along, cause as soon as we get on Parris Island every dang thing we own will be mailed back home. All, even our toothbrush. Everything will be anew, like being born again. Did you tote a lot with you?"

"Naw, a couple t-shirts and an extra pair of khaki pants. Is your Dad and uncle ex-Marines?"

"Yepper. I turned 17 and got myself outta high school. I went to some kin in the mountains for a spell but brought some troubles on myself and went back to Weirton. My Dad told me to join. Said it will do me a world of good. What about you?"

"I quit too. Didn't finish the tenth grade. I hated school." Bat said. "Felt like I was tied to a desk when I just wanted to roam outside.

"I know that feeling. I sat right next to a big window. I gazed outside more than at the blackboard. Why did you join? Your kin ex-Marines?"

"Naw. I quit school at sixteen. Got a job at a scrapyard separating metals for the mill but I got fired. I was just loafing around and disappointing my Mother. I went to the Army recruiter and asked to register for the draft early before I turned eighteen but was told I couldn't do that. The Army said I could only enlist at seventeen if I joined for four years. That seemed like an awfully long time for me. The Marine recruiter said I could join for three years, so here I sit talking to you."

"Why y'all get yourself fired?"

"I hung out at a neighborhood drugstore with some buddies. It had a soda bar and we'd hang around smoking, looking at girls, and licking ice cream cones. Then some in the gang got cars and we'd cruise for girls and start drinking beer. After a night of drinking I could never get myself up for work. Especially on Monday mornings. I got fired."

"I never drank beer. In the mountains I'd go running the ridge with my pals and don't drink soda pop unless sipping it with white lightning."

"Running the ridge? What's that?"

"Outside. In the wilderness.

"My grandpa made wine in his cellar." Bat said. "It tasted pretty good. I never tasted homemade whisky."

"It sure ain't sweet wine." Smoky laughed. "Drinking white lightning all night makes you simple minded."

"Did you get in serious trouble back home in the mountains?"

"Yep, a real mess of peas." Smoky showed a sad face. "I get the sorrows thinking about it. Keeping that time to myself."

"Oh, for sure." Bat blurted. "I didn't mean to pry."

"I pray over my troubles." Smoky hung his head. "You know Jesus Bat?"

"Well, yeah, I do."

"I see a shining Papist medal around your neck. Until I settled in Weirton I never knew a Papist. Folks in the mountains claim Papists pray to idols."

"I don't pray to idols." Bat grinned. "Papist? I'm Roman Catholic."

"Aw, I knowed now. I made some catholic acquaintances in Weirton who told how it works, some kind of intercession they said. Sorta like begging a sainty dead friend agone to Jesus to pray for needs."

"Yeah, it's not complicated, at least not after the nuns explained it in school. I'm not a good Catholic like my mother but I know we don't pray to idols."

"I knowed I'm not so well a Christian either. Never did take to them holier than thou folks. Catholics got some folks like that too?"

"Yeah." Bat nodded. "I suppose those types are everywhere."

"Our folks meet and sing and dance." Smoky gave a wide grin. "Read the Good Book. Get themselves all worked up, waving arms and stomping about. It's a sight to behold."

"Oh I know what you mean." Bat said. "We call them holy rollers."

Smoky faced Bat. "Holy Rollers don't test faith like my Ma's folks. I'm speaking of fearless faith, snake handling and drinking poison. Scare ya out of your britches going to my Ma's church. Like the Bible sez, take up serpents, drink poison, have faith, be believing."

"Snakes? What sort of snakes?"

"Timber rattlesnakes. Copperheads."

"Have you?"

"Took up serpents?" Smoky sighed. "My folks are of two minds about praising the Lord. My Ma's kin follows snake handling preachers. Pa's kin sez it's testing God. The good book warns not to be putting the Lord our God to a test."

"So you follow what your Dad practices?"

"Yep." Smoky grinned. "I'm not ready to be shaking snakes for Jesus. My Pa's Church of God does all the rest, the singing; shouting, dancing, talk in tongues, but no snakes or poison."

"Your Mother drinks poison? What kind of poison?"

"It's more like sipping it out of a jug. Strychnine."

"I'd like to see that service." Bat said. "Sometimes our Mass is boring. Depends on the priest."

"Hell spells Bat. I'll invite you right now for later on when our training days are over. My folks will welcome any friend of mine."

Bat smiled. "Perhaps someday Smoky, but I ain't handling snakes."

"No need to. Folks who have fear and doubt told not to partake unless living correctly and having total trust in God's Will."

Bat sat perplexed that people handled poison snakes and drank poison during worship. He'd never heard of such practices. He studied Smoky for a few moments for any telltale sign that the mountain boy was stringing him along with some sort of hillbilly prank. The slim tall teenager sat quietly goggling the grand concourse of the train station and every now and then would make a comment about the beauty and largest of the station.

"Ever think you'll handle snakes?" Bat quizzed.

"Nope." Smoky laughed. "Taking my Paw's advice. Only handling the snake in my pants."

Bat laughed hard with him. They were bonding.

"Yer folk's churchgoing?" Smoky asked.

"Mon is a member of the Blue Army?'"

"Never hear of a Blue Army."

"It's not really an army. Only name members go by. They don't dress up in blue or march around anywhere. About what happened at Fatima?"

"Fatima?"

"A village in Portugal."

"What happened?"

"Mary appeared to three village kids. Told them some secrets and predictions and her visits went on for months to those kids. And something strange happened with the sun. My mother has a newspaper clipping showing the tens of thousands of people that said they saw the sun spinning. I haven't read about it as much as my Mom wants me to, but someday I will."

"You speaking of Jesus' Mom showing up out of nowhere?

"Yeah." Bat said, nodding his head.

"I reckon I'd like to read those clippings myself. What does she predict?"

"She said things about the two world wars and about the spread of communism in the world. Communist Russia would fail and go away if people prayed the rosary. That's what the Blue Army does. They meet monthly in groups and pray together to halt the spread of atheist communism like Mary requested."

"Fellowship we call it when neighbors gather up in a house. Pray and read scripture. My kin fellowship a bunch. Often my Ma, bible in hand, dragged me to fellowship. But I sure like to hear more about that Portugal place someday."

"I should learn more about it myself." Bat uttered while wanting to get off the Fatima subject because he knew so little about the event himself. "Do you have a steady girl Smoky?"

Smoky hung his head. "I did till I brought on my troubles. Don't know if she'll come around to see me in the future." He brushed away at his watering eyes and Bat quickly changed the subject again.

"Did the recruiting sergeant in Weirton tell you any details about our train trip to Parris Island? Mine told me nothing except to meet him here and not to pack much."

"We'll ride a sleeper car to Washington D.C. We'll be changing trains there for the rest of the trip." Smoky answered but still had his sad troubles and girlfriend in his thoughts. "Her name is Ursula. I sure do miss her Bat."

Bat sat silent staring across the grand concourse at the people coming and going in and out of the train station. He'd poked a nerve in his new friend that brought his sad brown eyes to water. He'd have to be careful not to bring up girlfriends or love till they got to know each other longer, and better.

14

"You have a girl Bat?" Smoky asked with his head hung down looking at his worn black shoes.

"No steady. Actually, to be honest I know two girls that make my heart flutter when I'm near them."

"My mind never wanders far from Ursula." Smoky confessed. "I can't picture a life for me without her in it. I just can't. My Pa may be right. The Marine Corps will do me a world of good. I hope so. I pray for it."

Bat felt a crushing sadness for his new friend while gushing out his willingness to pray for Ursula's return to his new pal. "I'll pray you get her back too." Then Bat felt somewhat foolish. He'd never prayed for the troubles of his teenager pals hanging out at the drugstore. By joining the Marine Corps perhaps he was changing even before he left Pittsburgh.

Smoky turned to him, showing a wide grin with a wink. "I may be needing you to cart me off to that Fatima place. Catch me one of them there miracles to get Ursula back in my arms."

Bat patted Smoky on the back. "My Mom has a sign over her bed with a message from Einstein." Bat paused, eyes closed. "Either you believe nothing is a miracle or everything is a miracle. That may not be accurate but it goes something like that."

Smoky chuckled. "Gee I must be a genius too. I always believed that."

The blue uniformed recruiting Sergeant was entering the grand concourse to send them off with their written orders just as the call 'all aboard for Washington DC and track number' was being broadcast over the station loudspeakers.

One behind the other Bat and Smoky followed close behind the Negro porter leading them through the Pullman sleeper car. Both Bat and Smoky would have been pleased to take the train ride

15

sitting in the blue upholstered seats in the open section of the Pullman that the Porter walked them through. Leaving the car open area the passageway narrowed considerably with little remaining room for passengers to pass by each other. The smart uniformed Porter slid two doors open and smoothly motioned each teenager to his own completely private quarters. With a broad smile the Porter nodded that he acknowledged and appreciated their thanks then left them to themselves.

Limited space between the bed, sink, and door left a small space for standing. It was no problem for the lean long bodies of the youth. Bat called out to Smoky in the adjoining quarters. "More than I expected for my first train ride."

"Bless me Uncle Sam." Smoky said. "Got a big window to look out too."

"Bat smiled. "I got a window too. I guess we better quit talking and get some rest. See you in the morning, Smoky."

"Yep." Smoky answered while closing his doorway shut.

Bat shut his door, quickly undressed then climbed under the crisp linen and soft blanket. He switched off the reading light hung on the bed frame. The train began to move. He was on his way toward a new life. Scared but determined to use the Corps to make available to him better opportunities than he'd been born with by circumstance. Turning toward the window he bunched up the oversized pillow and gazed out watching Pittsburgh and Western Pennsylvania go by in the night.

Smoky wasn't sleeping or undressed. With his worn shoes off he stretched out on the cot. By the glare of the reading lamp he peered now and then at the wallet size picture of Ursula in his long fingered hand. Misbehaving and not listening to his elder's heaped trouble on his chances to someday marry Ursula. Her family got mighty angry at him for killing the baby and dang near Ursula too. If he'd only had listened to Ursula's Ma none of the troubles would have come about. She was warning him about climbing far out on tree limbs like a monkey toting a loaded gun but he wouldn't listen to her sane advice and made a mess of peas out of his life. So messy he couldn't finish his schooling with and near Ursula and joined back up with his parents in Weirton. Now he was on a train that was speeding him even further away from her. With the baby gone she went back to finish up her high schooling where there was plenty a boy there to meet up with and chase after her. His eyes began watering and he thought to himself that he'd be better off if he'd broken his neck when falling out of that sour green apple tree.

His picture of Ursula wasn't a portrait type photo he desired. It was a quick snapshot of her from the back of his uncle's old pickup truck as he was being driven away from her to the Greyhound bus stop near that small town's municipal building. In the picture she's standing next to her Pa in his working overalls. She is wearing a simple cotton dress, not waving goodbye or smiling, only staring his way at him sitting on his battered suitcase inside the rusty bed of the moving truck. His eyes were bleary with sadness when he clicked the photo and he worried at the time he'd missed her in the lens. She'd been back home from the hospital nearly three weeks and looked as wholesome and pretty as ever he'd seen her. He looked at her picture again holding it closer to the small reading lamp. Her long light brown hair was bunched and tied up in the back and she was standing barefoot on that dusty dirt road outside her folk's farm house.

He turned on his side toward the window and saw his reflection on the glass. He reached out and switched off the lamp light. He didn't want to see himself and was wishing he'd packed along his bible. Reading the good book relaxed his mind and offered him hope. He'd be certain to tote it with him after his training days were over and he was settled in at a permanent camp. He put Ursula's picture under his pillow, closed his eyes and wished for sleep.

A noisy streaking blur of light streamed past the window from a train traveling in the opposite direction startled Bat out of his light sleep. Near daybreak the train was scheduled to arrive in Washington, D.C. At the capitol the Recruiter explained he'd change to the Southern Atlantic railroad line for the remainder of the trip but that it would not be a sleeper. Not having a comfortable sleeper wouldn't be a problem as he already knew that the closer he got to Parris Island the more his nervousness would stop him from even dozing now and then. He started thinking about his family that he was leaving behind. Especially his mother and the sacrifices she made for him and the rest of the family.

When he'd left his home in the Flats for the train station she was crying. His father was stoic but Bat could see that beneath his controlled feature of suppressing his emotion his Dad was sad to see him go. Neighbors living in the Flats gathered on the brick courtyard to say farewell and wish him good luck. Some of them had sons of their own in the armed forces and understood a mother's sorrow when sending a boy off into the unknown. In that open area surrounded by the three storied wood framed flats the women often gathered and exchanged cups of sugar or flour or whatever was needed to help one another meet their needs for the day. The American dream of a better way of living had passed by Bat's closest neighbors and fellow tenets of the Flats long ago.

He would miss his family but felt certain that he'd made the best decision by leaving home. Factories weren't hiring with the recession and he was heading for trouble when friends around him began to take to alcohol and he joined in boozing along with them.

And with two younger siblings also at home and little money coming in he was just adding to his mother's woes. The booze had taken hold of his Dad years before and now advancing into middle age he was incapable of working a meaningful job. Now and then he'd get a brief part time job cleaning up a bar but most often he sat at home reading and sipping cheap wine to control his shakes and doing the household chores. A quiet man who loves to read the newspaper and keep up with the events in the world. Yet a man, a husband and father, that remained in a permanent depression by longing for a better start in life.

The oldest of nine he was sent off to labor early by his German immigrant parents to contribute to the family needs. He wasn't bitter about missing out on schooling and quite understanding that that was the way it was back then, but he still dreamed of what could have been had he obtained a higher education.

Bat's mother shouldered the family needs as cleaning women for people better off in other parts of Pittsburgh. Now and then he went with his Mom to clean houses. They would take the streetcar and she would point out nice homes along the way. During the Christmas season how glad she was when the better off families decorated their homes elaborately. She enjoyed seeing the holiday lights that she could not afford to display but was never jealous. Once he'd said that he wished for the same sort of bright Christmas. Be thankful she taught him for the people that can and do brighten their homes for us to see and enjoy. Be thankful you have eyes to see for some in the world who are not so fortunate. Be thankful for old worn shoes because some have no feet. Being thankful to God under every situation was her constant answer for daily living. And trust in Jesus and never stop trusting until your trusting days are over and your remains are lowered into the grave. Her life was nothing other than giving her all and forgiving to all. Taken to a catholic orphanage at age five after her parents both died only weeks apart from the swine flu epidemic of 1918 she never obtained the desire to have a better lifestyle at any cost if it meant offending God.

Now the further the speeding train took him away from his mother the more he began to recognize her influence on his character. He thought it strange that at the train station he said he'd pray for Smoky, a stranger without even being asked too. Something he never did much of on his own without being asked to do so by his mother. Pray for some poor soul, or for the Pope, or just about anything or anyone else that she believed needed God's intervention.

He always claimed he would pray when she asked but most often he didn't and when he did, the prayers were brief rote prayers he'd learnt in catholic school. Prayers quickly and silently said so that his mind could get back to thinking about things that really mattered to him, like getting honest money into his pocket or images of the girls that made his heart flutter. But now alone and scared he'd already prayed as sincerely as he'd prayed as a seven year old when making first communion. He pulled the covers over his head and said a prayer of thanks to God for meeting up with Smoky and hoped that they would both be successful at Parris Island and remain pals for a long time. In the dark warm bed he started praying the rosary using his fingers in place of beads since he hadn't brought a rosary along. He didn't have the slightest idea where his communion rosary was but felt certain his Mother would know its whereabouts.

Thoughts of Ursula weren't letting Smoky sleep or even doze off momentary. Images of her bombarding his mind seemed clearer in the dark room of the Pullman. Loving images of them kissing, walking, talking, and making love came hovering in his thoughts one after another like a flickering Hollywood movie. With the wanting thoughts also came the unwanted of what he had done and the cause of his painful heartache. If he'd only obeyed Ursula's Ma his life would've stayed the same and he wouldn't be aboard the train speeding into a different life. He curled up into a fetus position and easily recalled each moment of that sorrowful sunny day.

It was only spitting distance to the outhouse from high up in the branches of the sour green apple tree. Inside the freshly red painted wood structure sat Ursula, five months pregnant, relieving herself while leafing through a merchant clothing catalogue. Now and then after biting into an apple his lips would puckerup. He'd chew on the bit of apple refreshing his mouth with its juice before spitting it out. Ursula's Ma never had him pick any sour apples for her baking needs and didn't mind him climbing about the old fruit tree branches. But that day she fussed much with his climbing while toting his .22 caliber rifle while hoping to pick off a squirrel on the branches of trees close by. She warned him that disobeying his elders would bring on a calamity. And sure enough her prophecy came to pass.

Climbing further out on the branch than he should've for his weight, then going into a panic when the branch snapped, dropping him onto the branches below. Grabbing panicky for a better grip on the leafy branches his rifle discharged and jerked free from his grip and fell to the ground. Dangling by looping arms around a branch he couldn't see the bullet hole his mishap shot put through the wooden outhouse.

It wasn't until Ursula came wailing and stumbling from the outhouse with a frightful look on her face and seeing her bloody swollen belly did he realize he shot his true love. Overwhelmed with fright he fell from the tree along with an abundance of hard green apples. It wasn't until he reached the water pump drainage ditch did his skinny bruising body take its last tumble and stop moving.

* * * * *

Bat and Smoky left the body count walking toward the command post talking about themselves. Captain Bat spoke first "How is Ursula and the kids doing?"

"Fine."

"Great Lady Ursula. You're a lucky man. I recall those moments inside the train station when we met and talked about girls we were leaving behind."

Smoky chuckled. "I recall. You spoke about two hometown girls.

"Hell Smoky, before I finished boot camp I was forgotten by every girl I ever kissed. Anyway, they never thought of me as a serious choice. My romances back then were more wishes than reality. But not you and Ursula. God bless you both. When you write to her tell her I send my best, and I appreciate her prayers for my safety. Also I think I finally found someone, and will be getting married after, and if I get out of this jungle."

Smoky smiled."Who would've guessed we would both make a career in the Corps back then."

"Never entered my mind then." Several Marines passed by saluting Bat.

"Who would have guessed that someday you would be commissioned and I'd be a Sergeant Major?" Smiling, they walked silent until reaching the headquarters compound. Inside the hut Smoky reported on the attack while Bat took notes.

"…..under strength Marines against what appears to be a North Vietnam army battalion…..the Marines battered the enemy…..killing over 100 and still counting, capturing 30, some wounded severely and may not make it…..over 100 enemy weapons were abandoned on the battlefield….Captain Bat wrote as fast as he could to keep up with Smoky describing the battle. He already had a layout of the battlefield having had the helicopter pilot circle the compound several times even having lone rifle shots at them as they circled the jungle.

The main compound, surrounded by an earthen parapet and three belts of barbed wire consisted of several old french old building, bunkerd and dug in fighting positions. Across the road the Army had some engineers who were positioned at the compound entrance…..the Marines all shared the same thoughts of troubles coming their way…. Marine reinforces were rushed to the compound overland but they were still outnumbered…..at about 0300 hundreds of enemy troops launched a human assault at the northwest perimeter…..they must have expected little resistance...but that is where the Marine reinforcements were positioned…..I think NVA expected little resistance…..Marines up on the observation towel spotted them gathering during the pretend truce so we were ready for their attack…."

Afterawhile Smoky finished the debriefing and they both sat quietly for a while. Bat broke the silence. "Of all the wars in America's past we have to serve in this one. I'm sick over what is occurring. The wealthy boys hiding in the Reserves, college exemptions and demonstrations back home. The conduct of the war, how it's being fought. We're fighting for a draw and with our hands tied."

Smoky looked at the sad face of his buddy but kept silent.

Bat kept complaining. "I was talking to some Air Force Thud pilots.Those poor bastards are so restricted in their missions over North Vietnam it's almost impossible to believe. President Johnsan and his administration are acting like cub scouts in their logic. The restrictions over bombing the North are so restrictive it is bewildering. Day to day targets to bomb are given by the President and Secretary of Defense. Thirty mile perimeter, no bombing around Hanoi, ten mile limits around the port of Haiphong Harbor. The pilots can see the Russian ships unloading the missiles and military supplies at the ports but aren't allowed to attack. Not allowed to bomb dikes, dams. Command and control centers inside no bombing zones. The only explanations I've been given for fighting a war this way is Johnson, so fearful of widening the war with Russia and China. Well with the rules for fighting this way we should all go home. Sorry Smoky for unloading my anger but it's terrible to bring American men over here year after year to die under these current conditions and rules of engagement."

"I agree with you, Bat. It's our misfortune to get stuck in this war. Maybe I will put it a different way. It's our misfortune to serve under President Johnson. He doesn't want to win and he doesn't want to lose. Politics is all they think about and their place in history. It's young boys like me and you were back at the Pittsburgh train station that's fighting and dying in this war, with the others getting deferrrements or running to Canada. Whatever it's worth, we came here not to conquer or pillage but to keep people free. We can take a bow and put a feather in our hat that our intentions are good. Freedom like we did for the South Koreans, but the rules for fighting this war have been bizarre."

Bat stood. I need to report back with your observations. They walked together to the helicopter. "Well Sergeant Major, any last words of wisdom before I leave. Any lessons learned from this battle that Command can forward back to the Washington politicians? A foxhole intelligent report?"

"Yeah, Smoky grinned. "Tell the President he has the enemy shitting their pants!"

"It's our history now!"

Hand Soap

Overdue Thank You
Ray Mall
"I overcame Ray"

Preface to Hand Soap

I favor Saint Augustian from among the saints. He best demonstrates to me with his struggling lifestyle Paul's solid preaching to the Roman's about "the pull of the flesh against the spirit." He wrote the Confessions about 397. For 16 centuries his numerous writings have been read, studied, and taught. Taught and lectured not only at divinity schools but also at the most prestigious universities of learning in the world.

Augie, the character of my short story, earnestly searches with his thoughts as Saint Augustine did for a higher purpose for his existence. Hidden reasons other than the desires for pleasuring his flesh, and seeking the companionship of well learned friends as himself. Identified as a leisurely lifestyle goal by fellow Roman Citizens of Augustine time.

After joining and participating with many sects or cults Augustine's intellect would ultimately reject those groups. Christianly, often being preached by far less educated persons and some Egyptian monks and dirty hermits stopped him from taking those desert christians called catholics seriously. Even his mother, Monica, a catholic convert, could not persuade him to Jesus. Nor could she convert Augustian's father, a pagan and low level Roman official in North Africa.

When he was about 30 he was offered a professorship in Milan to teach rhetoric and there he heard the sermons of Ambrose, the Bishop of Milan. His conversion to Jesus wasn't sudden, but it began in Milan with the voice of Ambrose and after a while he converted, became a catholic and smothered the world with his brilliant writings.

Augie, my Hand Soap story character, loves Augustine. He longs to return to his catholic roots and become a modern day Augustine helping the church during hedonistic modern times. He's living as a hedonist, self-indulgent, pleasure-seeking, pleasure-loving, and is tormented as Saint Augustian's was by believing there had to be more to life than fast living sensual conduct. Was King Solomon right on! "life is meaningless unless one lives it in the fear of God.

Keeping his commandments and enjoying life as a gift from Him"

However Augie has a problem. Saint Augustine as a pagan stumbles onto a fresh second look at christianity by a chance overhearing about the great rhetoric of Milan's Bishop Ambrose. Whereas Augie, baptized as an infant to Christ the redeemer seeks signs from God to return to his faith to take up Jesus' way seriously.

Will God give him a sign?

Hand Soap

"Hand soap! Dreaming about soap? How long have you been having soap dreams?"

"Two weeks."

"Antibacterial?" Giggling.

"Go on, laugh. I'm concerned. Could it be some sort of message?"

"From whom? God?" Laughing at me. "Okay, okay." Chuckling. "Open up. Give me the dreamy details."

My concerns over bothersome spiritual dreams while parking alongside a brightly lit strip club were nagging me. How far away from faith I drifted since dropping out of Trinity Jesuit College. I lost my way. I didn't stop loving Jesus, Only ignored his teaching since leaving the structural discipline life at Trinity. Do I love Jesus when I ignore him? Is that even possible?

"After work we'll talk." Feeling kindly referring to her strip-dancing as work.

"No. No. Now! My dance is an hour away and you're off work tonight. You're in some sort of cloud lately. At the apartment. Here at work. Talk to me. Get yourself out of the clouds. Feet back on the ground."

I won't answer her but she keeps jabbing at me to expose what I've been brooding over for weeks. I kept staring into her alert blue eyes. Her features were set in stone. She wasn't going anywhere till I talked. In a few hours she'll be slithering about a pole on stage wearing only glittering pasties on her nipples and a G-string. Men will be lusting after her. That was her job to bring forth lust, one of the seven deadly sins to the forefront of a man's mind. And my job? To bartend and serve alcohol to titillate their impious experience further along, or perhaps if they are married, with children, to help drown their conscience about where they should be, like at home with the wife.

Closing my eyes. Rubbing my face felt good. I am tired looking and need a shave. Everyday routine things I put aside as if being in a trance, pestered continuously by how I am living my life. Living until recently was full of fun with beautiful Eve at my side. Making plenty of money and loving it. Making money wasn't the root of all evil. Loving money is the root of all evil, the good book sez. Two weeks into my recurring dreams is leaving a spiritual torch burning within me. Questioning my way of living is taking its toll on my body. Am I being born again as Jesus preached? Saved? Pressured into being born again? I'd abandoned those sorts of ideas years earlier when I walked away from Trinity and joined the fun crowd. "Okay." I rubbed my face hard again. "Let's talk."

Shifting in her seat. "Good. I hate living with a corpse. They always decay."

"It started two weeks ago. I dreamt I'm entering the chapel at Trinity College and going to cross myself with holy water. But, instead of holy water inside of the fount there was a bottle of golden colored hand soap. In my dream I was startled but I entered the chapel anyhow without touching the hand soap, knelt and prayed. After I finished my prayers I looked around the chapel. It was bejeweled with paintings, statues of saints, artistic adornments by artists revealing a love for God through imaginative expression. A thoughtful revelation was placed into my head while looking at the statues. All of the saints are not fully clothed, undressing. Then suddenly the statues of the saints are wearing bikinis or G-strings and pasties. Their stone heads are shaking and wagging their fingers, no, no, no! I woke up."

"Wow! Wow! Wow! I'm traumatized. Strippers are on their own, no patron saint to pray too. Unfair! I Thought Papists had a saint for every trade. I don't get a patron saint? So disappointing. Do whores?"

"See your response! That's why I wanted to wait, talk tonight. After work."

Moving her long fingers across her full pink painted lips as if zippering them shut while motioning with her hands and arms for me to continue. Feed her more about my dreams. I know that it won't be long before her month will unzip. "That was the first night dream. Since then I only dream of the fount filled up with golden liquid hand soap. No bottle."

"How do you know it's hand soap? It could be ginger ale. Perhaps job related. Bartender treat? Help yourself to a highball." Couldn't control herself. Sniggering.

"It's hand soap. In the first dream it's in a bottle lying inside the chapel entrance fount and labeled in clear white letters. Hand soap. After that dream no more bottles, just a fount with glittering golden hand soap."

"Did you cross yourself with it? Huh? Smiling, lifting her eyebrows.

Getting nosy. Wanting to know more. A big fan of television crime shows, a serious reader of crime novels, I could see her attitude toward my dreams changing in her widening bright blue eyes.

"No. A chill comes over me at the fount and I enter the chapel. Genuflect. Enter a pew and look around. All the statues of the saints are gone now in the dream except one. A woman figurine placed on the altar and written in bold dark letters on its base is the name Monica. It's terrifying and then I woke up."

"Do you know a Monica? Have you ever known a Monica?"

Gently rubbing my whiskers mumbling between my fingers. "Not in real life."

" What sort of answer is that?" Frowning. "What other life is there?"

"Spiritual."

She shifted in the seat. "Here we go back in time, into your catholic upbringing. Until a few weeks ago, before this soapy dream of yours, you were a fun guy. Living as if nothing else mattered except having fun. Making easy cash to have more and more fun. I never heard you question our mode of living except, and don't take what I'm going to say wrong, but..." Hesitating.

"Go on. You won't hurt my feelings."

"Ok Augie, I think it's your Mother putting guilt feelings on you. The only time I see you glum, go into a short time depression is after you visit your Mom. Or, talk long on the telephone with her. Your conversations with her are all spiritual. You told me yourself how she constantly prays for you to return to God, and for me also to find Jesus. Take my hand Augie. I Love you. You're a good guy with friends that love you. Always willing to help anyone, but your Mom is a little touched in the head?"

"Perhaps she is but weren't most saints?"

"Don't ask me. I know nothing about saints."

"Jesus said about John the Baptist that no greater man was born of women, and yet today our society would have him institutionalized. Could you imagine him standing on a sidewalk in a modern city screaming at politicians and people to repent?"

"Oh," perking up. "I know about him. He's the dirty one standing in the river that baptizes people. I saw it in the movie. It's always on television at Easter time."

"Why God do I love her?" Mumbling to myself. Bright mind. Intelligent, but lacking a worldly wise education. Wonderful example of a non-challenging public education system. "Yeah that's him. He ate honey and bugs."

"Really?" Grimacing.

"I know I've been moody lately and I am sorry but this dream is making me crazy. I feel certain I'm being told something. Perhaps my mother's prayers are being heard. Or answered! With this statue of Saint Monica appearing in my dream, well it blows my mind to be truthful."

"Who was she?"

"The mother of Saint Augustine. My mother's favorite saint. She'd been pleading to Saint Monica for her intercession. For me to see the light. Forgo my sinning ways. Be saved."

"Hold up! I need to get this story straight. The mother and son are both saints?"

"Yeah. He's a great saint. A doctor of the church and recognized by all of the mainline protestant churches also as a great Christian teacher. A defender of the faith. I'd guess that a philosopher would reject his title if he hadn't studied Saint Augustine's great works. The Confessions, The City of God, and much much more."

"And you think your Mom's begging is paying off?"

"It's possible. Could be."

"Oh my God!" Covering her open mouth. "Your mother named you Augustine because Saint Monica named her son Augustine!"

"Yeah. And there's more about my dreams that's driving me looney. Listen to me. You might learn why I'm concerned.

"Ok ok, enlighten."

"For instance Saint Augustine wasn't always so saintly. He was a fun guy. Before being converted to Jesus's way he was at least a playboy, and probably a whoremonger. He loved the girls. Along with his buddies he boasted on his sex life. He was born in northern Africa around 350 when Christ's teaching was being challenged by many cults and religions. His father was a pagan, a minor official of the Roman Empire. His mother Monica was a Christian. In his confessions he writes how she labored with prayers continuously for her husband and son's awakening to the teaching of Jesus. Her prayers weren't answered quickly but she persisted in her petitioning. Over time her son converted. He became a great christian writer and teacher for God."

Her cosmetic made-up face for a stage and pole performance wasn't smiling at me. Or smirking, only staring at me as if I were someone she'd never seen before. Wide stares. I continue enlightening.

"Today, centuries later, educated christians of all persuasions praise Augustine's intelligence. His capacity to intellectually confront those during his lifetime that dismissed Jesus' way as false and only a passing cult."

Throwing her hands up high enough to strike the roof of the car and turning her face away from me, peering through the windshield. Gazing at other dancers walking over the parking lot to the back door entrance of the club marked in bold red letters. Private.

Puckering her lips. Deep breathing. Blowing air sounds. "Okie-doke! Let's see. We're talking about some guy, along with his mother, that wrote stuff 1700 years ago? A playboy. A man who lusted after women's private parts, but still became a saint that everybody with good brains likes."

"Yeah. I feel most do like his writings. He confessed that he was a slave of lust."

Screaming at me. "Oh my God he was a normal guy! I see my audience's lusty stares with every dance I do. Males are pushovers, like wind up robots when female concealed body parts are flashed bare at them. So this namesake of yours was acting normal Augie, like a regular guy until he went nuts over Jesus. Is that what you're telling me?"

"Somewhat like that."

"Whew." Loud exhaling. Lecturing. "It was totally like that. He was like you. He was smart like you. He liked women like you. He probably was handsome like you. He had a crazy mother like you. A nagging mother that wouldn't let him alone to live a life to enjoy. The only difference I can grasp between you and this Augustine saintly guy is you have a steady girlfriend that loves you."

"Actually, he had a longtime lover. Even had a son with her."

"Comparisons end with a girlfriend. Is there anymore?"

"Yeah. What I told you so far is only the beginning. It seems that after I fully absorb the meaning of the repeating dream then the dream changes a bit. Not much, just a bit. Stonefaced Monica's arms are spread wide apart when she first appears on the altar as if she is welcoming me back to Jesus and the church. After I grasp that message the dream changes a tad by giving another message." I stopped short of telling her of the message.

Shaking her head as if awakening her brain after I mesmerized it with crazy babble. Her blond ponytail flopping about and momentarily my maleness desiring to reach out to her, kiss her, caress her, and touch her hair, but resisting.

"Are you telling me I am a very bad person because I drop some clothes and dance around a pole showing my booty? And you are just as bad because you hang out with me, sleep with me, laugh with me, have fun with me. Is that what this Monica dream is telling you?"

"I'm not saying that. Did I say that?"

Eyes widening. "Not yet! What we do working at the club isn't that awful. Who do we hurt Augie? Ask your saintly mother that."

"I have! Said the strip club isn't that bad. No Sodom and Gomorrah, just somewhat mature entertainment."

"And what did she say?"

"Asked if I would take a nun there as my guest?"

"What a laugh. What did you say?"

"What could I say? There was no answer to give to her. If I said yes I'd take a nun we'd both know it was a lie. If I said no I will not take a nun to see you strip she would ask why not?"

"So what did you say?"

"My silence was my answer."

"Wow. She plays rough." Seeing a brunette walking across the lot I hear Eve opening the door window. Shouting out. "Margie"

Margie sashaying to us. "Hi guys. What's up?"

"Margie, will you be a Honey and do the first performance tonight? I'm in the middle of a chat here with Augie over something that needs to be talked out."

"Sure Honey. I will miss eyeballing you behind the bar tonight, gorgeous." I acknowledged her remark, forcing a smile and watching her walk away moving with the grace and lure of a Jezebel.

"What are you staring at Augie? If it's what I think it is, it'll be bare on stage in an hour."

"I've seen Margie's bottom plenty of times. Not a big deal to me." Coughing,

"Starting to choke on that lie Saint Augie?"

"Just clearing my throat. Ok ok! Now you see. That's the conflict raging in my mind. How the hell did Augustine go from a playboy to a saint? Overpowering lust? Control it?"

"Maybe he didn't." Questioning. "Only pretended."

"Not likely. His change of life is too well documented. Also the great Bishop of Milan, Ambrose, confirmed and baptized him into the church. He was the real deal Eve. Besides, people being strong in faith in Jesus is not unknown or even rare. Many have died for their faith in Christ. Fed to lions. Beheaded. Peter and Paul, other apostles. The Christian Church grew and blossomed from the blood of its martyrs."

"Gosh," touching my face gently. "Your Mom put a ton of gummy guilt on you."

Softly kissing the tips of her fingers over and over again while gazing past her through the open car window. A late April evening breeze was blowing into the car and it felt refreshing on my grumpy face. "Guilt is a symptom. My problem is finding the culprit causing the guilt."

"That's easy." Pulling her hand away from my lips. "Your cracked Mom."

"Perhaps. But I've been thinking. Couldn't my sins be the culprit? Think about it. When people, most people, do something they know they shouldn't do, like steal, cheat or speak lies they feel guilty. If not feeling guilty they most certainly agonize and fear over being caught. Fretting over being caught is a sort of guilt."

Stop lecturing to her. I started thinking. Sitting quiet, immobile, peering through the windshield. Neon signs blinking on the club roof, Girls! Girls! Girls! Enticing the world's dudes to come and lust! Lust! Lust! Lust until they're out of money, or until I announce the last call for alcohol from behind the bar. The colorful light reflecting off her beautiful features stirs' my own lust. How blessed am I to have her in my life, in my arms, and her love.

"And Stone Faced Monica is still sending you messages?" She asked me while placing her hand beneath a thin white sweater adjusting bra. Her bent red slack leg on the seat.

"By banners from one open hand to the other. In the beginning Monica's open arms and hands were inviting me to return to the church, now I see a white banner with word references stretching from one hand to another. I can see the dark words clearly and it's worrisome." Looking at her ankle and high heeled foot dangling over the edge of the seat I'm wondering if I should even be telling her about my dreams. Dreams that I could easily understand but she wouldn't without a scripture lesson. "I'd feel better talking to you back at our apartment about what's going on in my head."

"I've just postponed my performance. Let's get this over with and quickly. Do you hear yourself? You just said Monica's open arms and hands are inviting you. It's a statue Augie! Is there a real statue of this Monica inside Trinity chapel?"

"No." Gripping her red high-heeled foot."

"Then it's not even a real statue you're talking about. Fantastic! A fantasy Augie. Fantasies I know about. I pour them into bug eyed male heads every time I shake my booty and breasts from the stage."

"It's not the same. I wish it was just a dream. I feel more convinced after each vision that I am being given a message. I'm sorry for putting you through this anguish and having to put up with me in my present state of mind. If it's any help to you please know that I love you overwhelmingly.

"I feel the same Augie about you. We both know our jobs are just about easy money so that we can live a good life. I think maybe it's time for us to start saving our money instead of blowing it away by partying and eating out most of the time. After all, we're pushing up against thirty. I want to marry you someday, Augie."

"You're right. It's time for us to grow up. The club offers us little other than fast and easy cash. We have no sick leave, no vacation, no health insurance, not even security. We can easily be replaced.'

"Yeah. When I get a few wrinkles on my butt who'll want to rubberneck me with some smooth butt eighteen year old wanting to take my place. The club would care less if I show up on stage or vanish."

Taking her foot onto my lap heaving a loud sigh. "Of course the alternative is probably a time clock for you and a desk job for me."

"Let's talk about our future later. Right now what about those dreamy word banners Monica is holding between her cold hands? What was the last message?

"Enter the narrow gate." Removing her shoe. Start rubbing her foot which she has me do often inside of our apartment. She brings her other leg up onto the car seat for me to massage that foot too. Trotting about the stage in steep high heels many times a week pains her ankles.

"That's it. Enter the narrow gate? What's that supposed to mean? Do you know?"

"Yeah, it's a gateway into the hereafter."

"Hereafter has a gate?" Widening eyes. Surprised.

"It's a metaphor, a representation of a way of life in the Christian belief on following Jesus' teaching and being brought into God's kingdom after death. A narrow gate is harder to pass through than a wider gate. Being a Christian is hard and difficult and following Jesus' way can bring ridicule and grief. Being a Christian is like squeezing through a narrow opening from this hard life into heaven. It's a hard way. The christian way, but easy to avoid by choosing the wider opening and willingly ignoring what Jesus taught. Wide is the gate for the crowd that goes along to get along and avoid commitment. Commitments Jesus requires from his true followers which often leads them to be mocked." Rubbing her foot harder without looking into her face because I'm thinking she's taking what I just said as a sermon.

"It sounds like something my Mom used to preach about churchgoers back home in West Virginia." She started singing softly "Mister Christian goes to church each and every Sunday but Mister Christian goes to hell for what he does on Monday."

"Your Mom was a bit bitter. Died hostile. We spoke about her before and how she seemed mad at the world including your relatives after your father abandoned you and her. That said, her quote is exactly about leading a double life which is convenient for people to avoid the hardships required of a Christian. Jesus is telling us to stay true to his teaching which is the harder path that leads through the narrow gate and salvation."

"And we're in the crowd sauntering through our life toward the wider for sinners only gate? Right preacher? That's us?"

"I'd guess that it would be checked off affirmatively. Should be too."

."Crowded together with the crooks, killers, whores, adulterers, cheaters, deceivers, and other sinners, the two of us are marching happily along and dumb as two cows being herded into a slaughter house."

"Well no. There are exceptions. People that never had the opportunity to receive the Word may be excused to some degree. However, that is an entirely separate field of study. But whores on the other hand Jesus claimed would see the kingdom of heaven before hypocrites. And a correction; Love. Me and you, we're marching along like a bull and a cow to the slaughter house."

"Okee dokee know it all! I have a better chance of being saved if I start doing tricks?" Widening her big blues and grinning.

"Whores are not hypocrites. They offer themselves up for cash without deception. Unlike their customers who sneak about in the shadows and after expending their lust become mondays' Mister Christian your Mom was so fond of singing about. Jesus is very condemning of hypocrites. There are many ways to be hypocritical. Jesus only uses whores as an example to flush out two-faced ways."

Pulling her foot away from my grip. "And you believe what you just said?"

"I guess I do." Murmuring without looking into her eyes. "No. No guess. I do. That's why I'm having this crisis of conscience, this war of scruples, these mind blowing dreams. If Jesus is who I believe he is, then following his teachings is the sane and good way to live. And to bring as many people, especially people you love along with you through the narrow gate and into eternal life. Common sense! That's what Saint Monica wanted for the son she loved."

"Common crap I say!" Sat up straight facing the windshield.

"It's not crap." Raising my voice somewhat reveals my disappointment by her thoughtless reply. "If the world's people lived as Jesus' taught it would be a wondrous way to live our days under the sun. No murdering each other, no stealing, no coveting, no cheating, no bearing false witness, honoring our parents, Thanking God for our very existence. And if we fail at times, repent, knowing that we are forgiven by God. That's not crap. That's the path to paradise."

"Oh yeah?" Snickering. "What about coveting? Huh? Huh? Did Jesus reveal how to stop coveting? Men covet me at every stripdance. All staring and coveting, staring and coveting like foolish naughty boys. Augie, without coveting," chuckling, "I can't earn a living so darn easily."

"I know, I know. Coveting is the trigger to bigger sins. Coveting left unchecked becomes alive in the soul, growing in desires before the rape, the adultry, the stealing, the murder. Coveting as a commandment seems a small sin compared to murder, stealing, adultery. A rule easily ignored as not very hurtful or harmful like some of the others. But it's the leader of bigger ways to offend God."

"Why do you think you're a good barkeeper?" Blurting at me. "I got news for you, it's not because you're a connoisseur of alcohol! It's because you're full of crap! Shit! All sorts of bullshit. Funny shit. Sports shit. Political shit. History shit and what I'm hearing now, holy shit. But most of all on the top of all your shity talents is your quick wit that makes customers laugh."

Nodding my head acknowledging. "But as hard as I try I can't shake these crazy thoughts and dreams. I'm going nuts and think God is calling me to do something special but won't tell me what it is until I submit into complete submission to his will." Eyes watering "Am I nuts or what? I don't know what to do."

Sitting silently thinking, and distressing. Saint Augustine had a long time girlfriend too before he gave up his carefree ways and parted from her for his new life serving God. Is that what my hand soap dreams are about? God calling me? Telling me to wash my hands of my sinful ways and be born again?

"Why would God pick you? A bartender in a strip joint? My Lover. A lover of strippers. A lover of many strippers before settling down with me and on me. Yeah he would? Sure! I doubt that!"

"It's not as mysterious as it may sound." Turning away from her. Staring at the outside blinking stripjoint lights. "It would be odd.

Hard for people to accept but it wouldn't be as if God hasn't made oddball choices before to have his will known."

"Quit it!" Threatening. "You're making me nuts too!"

"I'm being truthful."

She lit a cigarette, turning away from me but I was feeling more and more that God is calling me, a lustful playboy perhaps but God's ways are not mankind's ways. And I knew that most modern christian preachers are not fanatical messengers warning of fire and brimstone for failing to repent. Maybe that is what God wants. Preachers that warn. Teaching the message of salvation to the indifferent and the worldly-wise is harsh enough on the messengers without hindering their work with rules that they cannot hurt anyone's feelings. Rules over emphasizing Jesus' loving image sometimes get in the way of Jesus' message. In much the same way that Jesus' miracles drew attention away from what he was saying. The multitudes were being caught up in the wonderment of healing instead of his words.

I reflected on the oddball men God had used in the past to serve his desires. John screaming out sins of politicians from a modern day street corner as the Baptist shouted out the sins of Herod wouldn't have his neck stretched over a chopping block today. But nevertheless he would certainly be silenced by heavy sedation and fitted into a straight jacket. Yet Jesus proclaimed John the greatest man born of a woman.

Eve's crossing her legs. So beautiful. So sexy. How could I ever do with her as Saint Augustine sent away his long time lover and started a life dedicated to God. I thought of other odd picks God used to get his way. Paul of Tarsus, a tentmaker, and stone throwing killer of christians before being struck blind on the road to Damascus to better see the light of Jesus' message of victory over death. In our hedonistic modern world, Paul would be relegated to an obscure evangelistic television station where he would be forced to huckster his tents just to afford broadcasting on a television network. When heaven wants authentic crazies like John and Paul, heaven will bring them forth, and probably from places we least expect or approve of with our narrow view of God. Perhaps another temperamental murderer like Paul, or a filthy recluse like John. A doubter like the apostle Thomas or a lustful pagan like Augustine. Maybe even a bullshitting bartender?"

Sighing, opening the car door. "Margie will drive me home. Get some rest Augie. Everything will be fine. I know you. I'll show you. Love you."

"Love you too."

Watching her walking away and entering the building I suddenly had an urge to drive about the desert roads of Southern California with no declared destination in mind. Like Augustine I too was born in the desert. Yuma. It was a clear sky night with a bright moon. Like Augustine I thought I could give up Eve and obey God's calling. What was happening in my mind kept hammering the same message. God's calling you but I wasn't certain it was really Him dialing or just a guilt in my brain. I turned on some classical music to mellow my soul. Listening to the music I moaned out loud to Augustine's spirit how I wanted to be like him. Write philosophy like him. Let the mob idolize the movie stars, the sport heroes and the super rich. Just give me the character of Saint Augustine so I could shine like the stars blinking forth great literature explaining the wonderment of Jesus our Redeemer.

I turned onto Interstate 8 heading east out of San Diego toward the Sonoran Desert. There was no traffic heading east. Unusual. Lighting up a menthol cigarette and trying to relax to the caressing sounds of mellowing music. Whispering to God. "Please give me a clearer sign."

After several Mozarts I decided to exit the interstate and head home back to the apartment. In the middle of the exit ramp hopping along in my headlight beams is a jackrabbit. A big eared hopping jackrabbit going forward without any concern that I was driving directly behind his furry ass. Blasting my horn but it keeps hopping at the same pace. I'm steering to the right of the animal but it's moving along with me to the right. I'm switching left and it's moving to the left. It's zigzagging along with me and my car and won't let me pass by his monumental eared body.

The killer instinct is not in me so I slowly follow behind. The desert pest is still in my path entering the ramp to go west on route 8. The ramp is overcrowded with jackrabbits stirring into my headlights.

"What the hell!" A field of lengthy ears pointing skyward. And now like Paul being knocked to the ground on the road to Damascus I get the message. Ears! God wants me to preach to the ears! Blasting my horn in celebration at receiving a sign so quickly the jackrabbits scattering from my sight. My hand soap dream? Wash my hands! Wash away my dirty way of living. It was clear as crystal now! Switching Mozert's genius for Handel's Messiah. Shouting "Hallelujah! Hallelujah!"

Exceeding speed limits to get home. Eve will be at the apartment now. I will break the news that God gave me a sign and as hard as it will be, we must part. I will imitate Saint Augustine and will turn my life around and study. Be a scholar for the Lord.

Entering our apartment I can hear the shower water running. Pacing the living room floor meditating on words to confront her about my calling, and how difficult it will be for me to live apart from her. I will be weak no longer. Live a life separated from her curves. Her charm. Her kisses and warmth. I should and could be a Saint Augustian. Expend all of my vigor, my vitality in pursuit of knowledge for the glory of Jesus Christ whom I love. And who loves me.

Showering water goes silent. "Eve, I'm home."

"I'll be right with you. Give me a minute. Are you hungry? I got a healthy snack for us."

"Yeah I am. A bit."

"Eat something before you get sick. You've been wasting away brooding. Unhappiness is a scourge."

I told her about the awesome congregation of jackrabbits.

"They're not really rabbits, Augie. The're hares. We have snowshoe hares in the Hills back home in West Virginia. Hares out this way have black tails. They do bunch up."

I was startled. I didn't know that, yet she did.

"They rest in groups, my grandpaw told me. Reckoning on the eyes and ears of one another for better protection. I thought you'd know that being from Arizona. The desert is overwhelmed with them."

Her hillbilly smarts bothers me even more now.

Entering the room bare. Bearing a fruit close to her painted lips. "Yummy snack for us." Eyes beaming mischievously like a Cheshire cat. Taking my hand. Leading me to our bedroom doorway. Hillbilly analyzing. "You're more an Adam than a Saint."

"God, *the bedroom doorway is fairly narrow.*"
"Listen to your Mum, Augie"

A Cherished Memory

Lou Pail
Pittsburgh's Alcoholic Anonymous' Apostle
"Miss you cuz"

Preface A Cherished Memory

Originally composed on single paper sheets as a tribute to Lou soon after his death in July 2015, I now decided to include 'A Cherished Memory 'with the publishing of 'Short Tales'. And a more permanent record of that disappointing day of rejection for Lou by the United States Navy. Now we all know he eventually found a better calling. Leading and helping many afflicted people away from alcohol and onto a better way of living.

Lou has also been honored with a plaque at Saint Paul's Monastery on the southside of Pittsburgh Pennsylvania for his efforts improving deteriorating lives. He desired to make AA participants live both a healthier and more spiritual life. He led many retreats to the monastery. A good place to pray, meditate, rest, and for some of Lou's extra special friends, a good place to dry out after falling off the wagon.

Lou was a Navy loss and Alcoholic Anonymous' gain.

A Cherished Memory

Imagine a morning in May with me and Lou Pail. We were jubilant that early spring morning back in 1955. We were also leaning on one another with imaginative talk to camouflage our uneasiness over what we were about to do to ourselves. Crossing the Allegheny River by walking over the sixteenth street bridge into downtown Pittsburgh we allowed our imaginations to travel on how our new lives would be. Certainly we expected adventure and danger. After all, we were headed to the old post building and signing up for duty in the armed forces of the United States years before we expected to receive our official draft notices. Lou was joining the Navy because his Dad had served as a sailor at one time in the past. I was set on joining the Naval Forces too, but as a Marine and to this very day I cannot fully grasp why.

For some strange reason, and even though we understood that once we shipped out of Pittsburgh we would be sent in opposite directions; Lou probably to the Great Lakes training facilities, and myself most certainly to Parris Island. Yet in our adventurous mindset we expected to see each other often. Most assuredly from time to time on the same ship, on the high seas, and would get sea sick? The Korean War had just ended against the communist North Korea in a truce but there were still plenty of Reds across the planet preparing to squeeze liberty to death. America and its armed forces had to stay prepared and vigilant. With all the unknowns ahead of us we entered the recruiting office and signed up along with a roomful of other teens filling out papers and waiting to be medically examined. And here is where we met Mister Hernia whom if he had not grown in Louis' groin many persons reading this true tale today probably would not have been born. Many more would not have entered Alcoholic Anonymous through Lou as their sponsor as he would have been off drinking from one exotic port to another and soon in desperate need of a Lou-like AA missionary himself. Would he have met sweet and pretty Carol Erb? Who would not have been born? How many UPS packages that Lou handled would have had to be delivered by someone else? Let's meet Mister Hernia.

The recruiters, Army, Marine, Air Force and Navy gathered us all into a herd of teens and guided us into a spacious room, ordered us to strip down to our underwear and line up in several rows facing them. As the others in the room we quickly obeyed our first official military order with gusto. We were all skinny; city teens from workingmen and ethnic neighborhoods. A mix of lads in clean and soiled underwear showing, and I guess now looking back not at all bright but willing to fight for the red white and blue anywhere in the world.

Down the line the doctor came facing each teen, administering a quick examination, listening with a stethoscope to body sounds especially with the heart and lungs. And then he'd put his hand in and around the groin area and give us our second order; turn your head to one side and cough. I and Lou were side by side. The Medical Officer stood in front of Lou and did his thing with the stethoscope, then Lou turned toward me and coughed. And that is when Mister Hernia made his entrance and changed Lou's future. The doctor scolded Lou in a loud voice, accusing him of trying to join the Navy so that he could get a free operation. Hernia operations in 1955 were more painful and had a much longer recovery period. What good would Lou be in the Navy lying around on his ass in bed for an indefinite time period? Lou got his last and final military order; Get dressed and get the hell out of here! Lou obeyed and Mister Hernia and him left the recruiting offices and waited for me outside.

I passed my examinations and was told to go home and await orders to Parris Island. Lou was living with my family at the time, his mother and mine were sisters. The walk home for a time was somber but Lou being Lou twisted his disappointment into some humorous teasing and tall tales. For certain the Marines were going to use me for cannon fodder. Why else would they take me? We bantered back and forth for some distance walking back to our tenement home on lower Tripoli Street on the Northside. Flats with its slanted floors, no shower, rattling windows, but full of people we loved and loved us. Some of them are very brokened people, the same sort of people Lou would seek and help through life while always leaning to God to get through each day. The tenements, or flats as some called them, had a lot of broken people for young minds to observe, and we did, and later in life Lou and I would have long telephone conversations on many subjects about the human condition.

Before we reached home Lou changed the entire event of the day around. With a twinkle in his Irish eyes he told me he knew he had a hernia, knew he'd be rejected, just wanted to get rid of me, out of our overcrowded tenement rooms, and get my softer bed. But the truth is I doubt if either one of us teen dummies accurately understood what a hernia was at that time in our life.

"A happy hereafter cuz."